WINNING WORDS

Sports Stories and Photographs

Charles R. Smith Jr.

CANDLEWICK PRESS
CAMBRIDGE, MASSACHUSETTS

CONTENTS

"STRIKE ONE!"

Here we go again. Why do I keep getting strikes? Come on, Bri. Let's get a hit and get out of this . . . this . . . don't you dare say that word, Brian. That'll only make it real. I can't remember the last game I got a hit. How did this happen? The season got off to such a great start. First a double, then a homer, then a bunch of singles, then a bunch more doubles. All in the first five games. But then all of a sudden . . . *WHAM!* Nothing.

Step out of the box. Deep breath. Fix helmet. Fix right glove. Strap off. Strap on. Tight. Fix left glove. Strap off. Strap on. Tight. Tap right cleat with bat. Tap left cleat with bat. Step back in. Right foot, scratch dirt. *Scratch-scratch-scratch.* Left foot, scratch dirt. *Scratch-scratch-scratch.* Swing bat. One time. Two times. Three times. Deep breath.

That last pitch seemed a little high. Maybe I should swing at the high stuff. Did I swing my hips all the way around? My hands were a little slow. Are my eyes going bad? Is the center fielder waving his arms at me? What's his name again?

"STRIKE TWO!"

Not again! One more strike and that makes oh-for-I-don't-even-*know*-how-many. I lost track of how many games it's been, but I think some of my teammates have gotten a little taller since I last got a hit. Frank, our best hitter, keeps telling me what to do to get out of my. . . . Don't say it, Brian. I keep telling him not to say the big *s* word, because sooner or later I'll get a hit. But when?

Step out of the box. Deep breath. Fix helmet. Fix right glove. Strap off. Strap on. Tight. Fix left glove. Strap off. Strap on. Tight. Hit right cleat with bat. Hit left cleat with bat. Step back in. Right foot, scratch dirt. *Scratch-scratch-scratch.* Left foot, scratch dirt. *Scratch-scratch-scratch.* Swing bat. One time. Two times. Three times. Deep breath.

I remember this pitcher now from the first game of the season. I put a good pasting on the apple that day, I did! I think I got a homer. Why's he up two strikes on me now? Am I wearing my lucky socks? Did I eat my lucky meal? I gotta-gotta-gotta have my mayo-and-pickle sandwich, two fried eggs, and pineapple soda. You know, Mom got this new low-fat mayo recently. I wonder . . .

"STRIKE THREE!"

Not again! Out number three. I toss my helmet into the dugout and grab my mitt. Time to play some defense over at third. Seventh inning. I still might get one more shot to get a hit. At this point, though, who cares? I just want this game to be over. So what if I never hit the ball again? Is that such a bad thing?

Just watch him and nothing else.

Who am I kidding? Of course I want a hit. I love to hit. I love hearing everybody cheer when I smack one into the field. I love making the pitcher's eyes look up to the sky when I launch a homer. I love all of that.

Anyway, it's over to third base, the hot corner. A lot of guys are afraid to play over here because things happen so fast. Yeah, you gotta be on your toes, but that's why I love it. If the ball is hit to you, it's gonna come hard and it's gonna come fast, but I love snatching it up to rob somebody of a hit. Maybe that's why Coach hasn't sat me down yet. My bat may be quiet, but my glove is still pretty loud.

"Ay batta batta batta batta battaaaaaaaa . . . Whaddya say there batta batta battaaaaaaaa . . ."

Come on, what's this guy gonna do?

A righty. I think he likes to pull. That means be ready. Always be ready. On your toes. Watch him and nothing else.

Strike two. Nice. He was swinging for the fences. Be ready for the next one. Always be ready. On your toes. Just watch him and nothing else. Punch the mitt. Punch the mitt. The mitt's hungry. The mitt's hungry. It's feeding time.

5

Crack! React. Here it comes. Lunge left. Leap. Stop. Off the dirt. Onto your feet. Throw to first. Got him!

That's the way. Out number one. Feeding time. Mitt's still hungry. What's the score? Down by two. Nobody on. Joey is on his game today. Next man is up. What's he gonna do? A lefty. I think he went deep to center last time. Doesn't matter. Be ready. Always be ready. On your toes. Watch him and nothing else.

First pitch. Swing . . . pop fly to first. Easy. Out number two. One out to go. My mitt has kept me playing, but it would sure be nice to hear the crack of my bat again. I gotta do something, but what?

Worry about that later. For now . . . next batter. What's he gonna do? Doesn't matter. Be ready. Always be ready. On your toes. Watch him and nothing else.

He swings. A hot shot, here it comes. React. One hopper on the dirt. Glove down. Stop it. Trap it. Grab it. Throw to first. Got him! Out number three. Sometimes I make this look too easy.

High fives await me as I trot back to the dugout, but Coach has his cap off and is scratching his head. Haven't seen that look on his face before.

"Great grab there, Brian. But listen," Coach says, standing near the steps. "Come here for a minute. I wanna have a chat with you."

We walk over to the far corner of the dugout.

"Sure, Coach. What's up?"

"Help me out, here, Brian. I just watched you make two tough plays on the hot corner look easier than breathing. Your eyes were so focused, you reacted like a fly avoiding a swat," he says.

"Thanks, Coach."

I punch my mitt.

"But I'm confused. I watch those same eyes of yours when you're up to bat, and it looks like your mind is dancing every-which-a-way."

He waves his arms around.

"Ummm, well, Coach . . ."

"I mean, it's like you're two different people out there. One of 'em is this kid punching his mitt, concentrating and waiting for the ball to be hit to him on defense." He took his cap off again and scratched his wispy gray dome before finishing. "The other is this kid with a bat in his hands and a look on his face like his foot is stuck in train tracks and the train is a-coming. Hard and fast."

I don't know what to say, so I say nothing. I just look away and tug on my cap.

"Alls I know, Brian, is that something ain't quite right when you got that bat in your hands. I'm not in that head of yours, so I don't know what's going on in there. Hopefully, you do. And hopefully you'll figure it out soon enough to get yourself out of that . . . " Don't say it, Coach. ". . . slump."

OH, NO! He said it. I can't believe Coach said IT. The big S. This is not good. Even though I've been in one, I've never said IT. Maybe I hoped that if I didn't say IT, IT wouldn't be real. But who am I kidding? Not only is IT real, it's my own private nightmare. But still,

Coach should know better than to use *that* word. He knows the code. He knows it's bad luck to actually say IT; especially in the dugout. Maybe he's just trying to fire me up by saying it. He succeeded.

I fling my mitt at the wall, and the *SMACK* turns everybody's head in my direction. I don't care. All I know is I gotta get out of this. I rewind my mind to my last hit, and all I remember is a *crack* and then a little white pill sailing through the sky, making the crowd cheer like crazy. I don't remember the swing or anything else. Just white sailing through blue. That was like a million strikes ago, though. Now, I just need one hit. Just one.

A few more bats crack, a few more mitts get fed, and we head into the ninth. We're the home team today, so we get last licks—and boy, do we need 'em. Jordan, Frank, Ronny, and maybe me.

Coach is up on the steps, looking at his scorecard and scratching that head of his again. He keeps glancing over at me sitting way in the back, and then he motions me over. Jordan draws a walk to first as I get closer to Coach.

"You know, Brian, as far as your . . . " Don't say it again, Coach. ". . . you know, goes, I noticed that when you're on the bag, you got this serious game face on, and you're all business. But when you got the stick in your hand . . . man, it looks like you're trying to solve some math equation. It's like you're not even there. Maybe if you approached the plate the same way you approach playing third, you'd get something going."

What? That makes no sense whatsoever. Playing third base is

SMACK!

defense. Swinging the bat is offense. How could they be the same?

"I don't understand, Coach. One is defense, the other is offense. What do you mean?"

"I mean, whatever is going through your head when you play third should go through your head when you're at the plate."

Cheers suddenly break out behind us on our bench, and then I see Jordan sliding into home to score. Coach looks me in the eye, grabs my shoulder, and simply says, "That means you're up."

Already? Jeez, I was listening to Coach babble so long that I didn't realize I was up. All right; since nothing else has worked so far, I'll try what he said. Even though it makes no sense.

Grab the bat. Down by just one now. OK, pretend like I'm going to the hot corner. What's this guy gonna do? Is it gonna be a fast ball? A curve? A change?

"STRIKE ONE!"

Uh-oh. Here we go again. Step out of the box. Deep breath. Fix helmet. Fix right glove. Strap off. Strap on. Tight. Fix left glove. Strap off. Strap on. Tight. Slam right cleat with bat. Slam left cleat with bat. Step back in. Right foot, scratch dirt. *Scratch-scratch-scratch.* Left foot, scratch dirt. *Scratch-scratch-scratch.* Remember, you're on the hot corner now, Bri. Swing bat. One time. Two times. Three times. The hot corner. Deep breath.

What's this guy gonna do? Doesn't matter. Be ready. Always be ready. On your toes. Just watch him and nothing else. React. *Crack!*

"STRIKE TWO!"

SO CLOSE! Foul tip! Aha! Now I think I see what Coach was saying. A little out in front on that one, but man, I haven't even had one of those in a long time. That sound! I wanna hear that again. Let's get something going here. Step back in. Deep breath.

What's this guy gonna do? Doesn't matter. Be ready. Always be ready. On your toes. Just watch him and nothing else. React. *SMACK!* The pitcher's eyes go up to the sky. Where's it going? Doesn't matter. GO-GO-GO-GO! First base; touch. *Huff-huff, puff-puff, huff-huff, puff-puff.* Second base; touch. Where's the ball? Right field. He's got no arm. KEEP GOING! *Huff-huff, puff-puff, huff-huff, puff-puff.* Third base is coming. Where's the ball? I don't see it. Where is it? Third baseman is waiting. His glove is up. I know what that means.

Slide! Legs first.

"SAFE!"

A triple! *Huff.* Yeah. *Puff.* That's. *Huff.* What. *Puff.* I'm. *Huff.* Talking. *Puff.* About. Tie game. But even better. *Huff.* No more. *Puff.* Well . . . you know.

Back on the hot corner: home sweet home. Man, it feels like I haven't been here in a long, long time.

"Concentration is the ability to think about absolutely nothing when it is absolutely necessary."

—Ray Knight

STUFFED EAGLES

"GO, EAGLES!"

CURT: Welcome back to AM twelve-thirty W-A-N-D's radio coverage of Anderson High School football. In today's matchup, we have your Anderson Eagles facing the Pottsville Beavers here in sunny Cedar Falls. It's a beautiful autumn day with temperatures hovering around the sixty-degree mark, and a light wind is whispering out toward the faculty parking lot. Down forty-nine to zip in the fourth and staring at another horrific loss, the Eagles teeter on the cliff of their most disastrous season in school history: no games won and no points scored. Their only hope now is to get on the scoreboard, and folks, that has proven to be a monumental task. I'm Curt Hamilton, handling the play-by-play for you as always, and seated next to me, color commentating, is one of Anderson's finest, the record holder for the most touchdowns in one season, Alvin "the Afterburner" Redman.

14

AL: Thanks, Curt, but you can just call me Al. Nobody's called me Alvin since short pants touched my ankles. Now, about this game. Where do I start? Jeez, these Eagles are most certainly getting plucked today. These hungry Beavers are giving them a pretty good shellacking.

CURT: As we mentioned earlier in the broadcast, Al, the Eagles have been plagued by injuries all year; their star quarterback, Joey Chipaway, was knocked out before the first game this season in a freak accident.

AL: I'll say it was a freak accident, Curt. Joey broke his hand while getting a high five from his offensive lineman, Terry "Tugboat" Saunders. And folks, Terry isn't called Tugboat for nothing. He towers over the grass at six foot three and tips the scales at a hefty 285 pounds. Poor Joey had no chance as Terry smashed his hand during the intro of the first game, screaming, "Go, Eagles!"

CURT: Talk about your bad luck, Al. That injury set the tone for the season. The Tugboat injured his knee moments later when he tripped over a kicking tee while trotting onto the field for the kickoff.

AL: Yup, Curt, these Eagles have been dropping like flies. I took a look at the injury report, and it has more names on it than after-school detention.

CURT: You've got that right, Al. All the Anderson Eagles have left now is a team of third- and fourth-string benchwarmers who are in for an uphill battle as they try to end the longest scoring drought in Anderson's illustrious history. Led by freshman quarterback Sammy "the String Bean" Grey, this group will try to accomplish something they have not been able to do all season long: get into the end zone and score.

AL: Boy, I tell ya, Curt, in all my time playing here at Anderson, I never experienced anything like this losing streak. My senior year, we went eleven and one, and I had at least one touchdown in *every* game. I remember my linemen opening up the hole for me, and *BOOM* — here comes the Afterburner, exploding past one defender, two defenders, stiff-arming another. . . . The end zone is in sight and —

CURT: Al, I hate to pull you out of the past, but back to the action at hand.

AL: Sorry, Curt. The air, the field, the crashing helmets . . . it always takes me back.

CURT: OK, Al. I was able to talk to Coach Carver at halftime, and this is what he told me about this bunch of youngsters. Punch up that audio clip for me, please, guys.

COACH CARVER: They may be third- and fourth-stringers, but they've still got pride. And in this game, that goes a long way.

AL: Indeed, Curt, indeed. Pride is a great motivator, but what will this group of youngsters show us in the fourth, Curt?

CURT: It looks like we're ready to kick off the tail end of the fourth and final quarter of this season, Al. The Eagles are at their twenty-five, ready to receive. The kick is up. It's a beaut. It catches the wind and drops to the Anderson twenty. It's caught by . . . Martini . . . excuse me . . . Martelli. Billy Martelli. He's to the thirty . . . the thirty-five and . . . WOW! . . . gets absolutely leveled at the thirty-seven yard line by . . . Gaines . . . Clarence Gaines of Pottsville.

AL: MYYYYYYYY GOODNESSSS, Curt! Martelli sure got his bell rung on that one! I'm surprised the ball didn't squirt free from his hands, considering the wall he ran into in Gaines!

CURT: I couldn't have said it better, Al, and for those of you just tuning in, that's "Freight Train" Gaines. And he has been wreaking havoc on the field all day. Clarence is a senior and has been an all-county tackle for the Beavers since his sophomore year. He laid quite a hit on the young fullback. Martelli is slow in getting up on his feet and appears a bit dizzy. You wonder, Al, how these kids can take the punishment that some of these bigger players dish out.

He's to the thirty . . .

the thirty-five

AL: Especially from a kid like Gaines, who stands a couple of milk shakes over six feet tall and weighs several dozen doughnuts on the other side of 250 pounds. But that's football, Curt.

CURT: Yet these Eagles seem to show no fear in lining up against him. Martelli rises to his feet and teeters a bit from side to side as he makes his way to the Eagle huddle, Al.

AL: Yeah, Curt, it appears the freshman fullback got to witness the dizzy birds firsthand on that tag from the Freight Train.

CURT: We are ready to resume play. Two minutes and twelve seconds remain on the clock, Al. String Bean Grey barks the count. Freight Train rushes in on a blitz as the ball is snapped. Grey hands it off to Martelli, cutting hard to the right. Gaines steams in, colliding with Martelli, who continues to drive his feet forward. Four more Beavers jump in to bring him down at the forty-two yard line. A determined five-yard gain on the play by the impressive freshman!

AL: WOW! Where did this kid come from? You know, Curt, Martelli reminds me a lot of me. Hard-nosed. Fearless. Strong. And his legs are like tree trunks and never stop moving toward the end zone. The main difference, of course, is that I got into the end zone more—a whole lot more.

CURT: As play resumes, there's been a switch, Al. Martelli is in at quarterback, and Grey is in the slot as a receiver. Martelli crouches behind the center and barks the count. Grey cuts left, hesitates, and breaks hard right as the ball is snapped. Gaines is coming up strong. Martelli backpedals. Plants. Bounces. Looks downfield. Grey is covered by a blanket of Beavers. Martelli scrambles out of the pocket and heads upfield along the sideline. He's to the forty-five . . . the fifty. . . . Gaines is charging in from the right. Martelli lunges . . . and is taken down by the Freight Train at the Beaver thirty-eight. First down, Eagles!

AL: Talk about no fear, Curt! I can't say enough about the youngster, except that he reminds me a lot of me at Anderson. Running through one defender, stiff-arming another on the way to—

CURT: Sorry to interrupt your nostalgia, Al, but with just under a minute left, about forty yards separate the Eagles from the record books. No team has ever lost every single game while also scoring no points.

AL: Sorry, Curt, I did it again. What can I say? This kid Martelli has the Afterburner itching for some playing time again on the old gridiron.

CURT: That's okay, Al. The Eagles continue to advance as Sammy "the

Stringbean" Grey comes back in at quarterback. We pick up the action deep in Beaver territory at the thirty-eight.

AL: Curt, you gotta wonder what Coach Carver will pull out of the old playbook. Where were these kids Martelli and Grey earlier? If these guys were playing at the beginning of the game, let alone the beginning of the season, who knows what heights the Eagles could have reached. And on top of that, *THEY'RE FRESHMEN!*

CURT: Freshmen playing well beyond their years, Al. Just thirty-five seconds on the clock. Chauncey Clark has reentered the game at the receiver position. Clark has made some great catches this year but has hurt the Eagles more by dropping passes at the absolute worst time. And that means nail-biting time for Eagles fans.

AL: I hear a few boos out there as Clark trots onto the field, but gimme a break! This is only his third game of the season, and he's another freshman just trying to fill in for this injured Eagles squad. Come on, Anderson faithful, how about some school spirit out there?

CURT: Grey steps into the shotgun formation. Martelli is wide right. Clark wide left. Grey takes the snap. Clark streaks out to the right on a diagonal. Grey bounces in the pocket. Gaines is charging hard from the right. Grey rolls to his left. Looks downfield. Martelli is covered tight in a zone. Clark is inside the fifteen and has some daylight between him and his defender on the right side of the field. Grey hurls a high one to Clark. Three Beavers converge in on him as he bobbles the pass. It bounces off his fingertips . . . onto the shoulder pads of a Beaver . . . onto the face mask of Clark and . . . into his hands. He made the catch! He made the catch! A thirty-two-yard reception for Chauncey Clark as he gives the Eagles a first down!

AL: What a catch by the freshman, Curt! That's the way, fellas. LET'S GO, ANDER-SON! LET'S GO . . .

CURT: Hold on to your helmet, there, Al. We still have eight seconds and about six yards to go. A pack of hungry Beavers separates the Eagles from the end zone. With their kicker out for the season, the Eagles will line up for one last chance at the end zone. It looks like we have another switch here: Clark is lining up at the quarterback position, Martelli is wide right, with Grey wide left. Gaines is lined up deep center on the one yard line as the last line of defense. Clark barks the count. The ball is snapped. Clark takes two steps to his right. Martelli takes the handoff, going to his left in the reverse. He races to the left upfield. And here comes Grey, sweeping down to his right, taking the handoff, completing the double reverse. Grey makes some headway to the two yard line. Gaines charges. Grey lunges his body toward the one yard line and . . . hold on . . . here comes Martelli pushing Grey. Am I seeing what I'm seeing? Half of the Eagles squad is behind Grey pushing forward.

AL: Wow, folks! I wish you were here to see this. The Eagles are all digging in to push Grey past Gaines and into the end zone. GO, EAGLES, GO!! PUSH THAT FREIGHT TRAIN!! PUSH THAT FREIGHT TRAIN. . . .

CURT: I think they hear you, Al. Grey's feet are inching forward as he and his Eagle teammates are plowing right through the Freight Train, and it appears that . . . hold on, folks. . . . The ref's hands are up and . . . it's official! TOUCHDOWN, EAGLES! TOUCHDOWN, EAGLES!

AL: SIX POINTS TO THE EAGLES! Well, how 'bout that turn of events, Curt? These Eagles just would not give up as they banded together to push back the mighty Freight Train. What can I say? I wish I was out there in the thick of it all, pushing and pounding and scratching and clawing and—

CURT: Yeah, Al. Anyway, the Anderson faithful are on their feet here, and you would think these boys just won the state championships, folks.

AL: Indeed, Curt. But these fellas deserve it. A bunch of third- and fourth-stringers nobody's even heard of kept this proud program from being a laughingstock in the record books. Their feathers may have been plucked, their beaks may have taken a pounding, but they never quit. . . . ANDERSON HIGH EAGLE PRIDE!

CURT: You said a beakful, Al. What a way to end the season, folks. Our time here is up. I'm Curt Hamilton, and alongside me has been the mildly energetic Al "the Afterburner" Redman, signing off on AM twelve-thirty, W-A-N-D, the home of the Eagles . . . saying good evening, Cedar Falls; we'll see you here next year!

"You are never a loser until you quit trying."
—Mike Ditka

"PASS IT!

Pass it! Wendy's open!"

Here we go again. Everybody's doing their own thing. We move the ball downfield and what happens? Nobody passes and we don't score. Again. Times like this, I wish I weren't the goalie. I wish I were the one taking the ball downfield. I'm glad to see Tara can get down there no problem, but if she doesn't pass the ball, who cares?

"That's it! That's it. Middies, open up a hole for Tara. Set her up. Wendy, watch the back."

So far the other team has scored one goal, and it was on a real nice play. One of them faked the shot and made me commit. Then she passed it off to her teammate, who knocked in the easy goal. Can't stop 'em all. At least we're only down by one. They must have been playing together for a while now, because they have that telepathy. You know, where they're all thinking the same thing and each one knows what the other one is gonna do next. We kind of play like that; the only difference is every time the ball goes to somebody, we all know it'll be a while before somebody else touches it.

"Nice steal, Megan. You've got Tara ahead in the left corner. Pass it off to Tara—she's got the shot. She's got the shot!"

NOT AGAIN! Megan makes a great steal, and what does she do? Ignores her teammates and gets the ball taken away. Again. But wait—at least Wendy got it back and is charging downfield.

"Wendy, what are you doing? Two people are open! Punch it right behind you for Megan."

Out of bounds to them? Ai-yai-yai! I don't understand this. We're so much better than them. Tara and Megan made all-stars the last three years in a row, and Wendy's the best ball handler in the league. I wish I knew how to dribble like her. Boy, can she go. She's like a snake out there. Slipping past a defender here. Sliding through a hole there. She makes it look so easy. I could probably do that too, if I spent every free minute I had kicking a soccer ball with my three older brothers like she does. I guess big brothers are good for something.

"Come on, Tara, get off the sidelines. Move to the middle of the field."

Tara . . . she's a completely different story. No brothers or sisters, but her mom played soccer in college and then as a pro in other countries, and I hear she was something else. Something must have rubbed off on Tara, because that girl has rockets in her feet. Some girls have a hard enough time shooting with one foot, but not Tara.

Not only can she shoot with both feet, but she can also hit the ball wherever she wants—hard.

"Megan, watch the back. Don't let them pass it behind you!"

Now, Megan . . . where do I start? That girl . . . whewww . . . she doesn't back down from anything. She has an older sister who plays basketball in high school, and they play together all the time. Her sister is always trying to get Megan to steal the ball. But, come on. . . . She's like six foot something, and Megan's not even five feet. That doesn't keep Megan from trying, though. Every time I go over there, they're finishing up a game of twenty-one or something, and Megan's just hopping around trying to take the ball from her tree of a sister. It's like a scene out of a movie, with her big sister holding the ball high above her head like King Kong and little Megan jumping around underneath her like a flea. I guess that's why she's our best defender; she finally has people her own size to pester.

"Great steal, Megan. Look upfield to Wendy. We can get a shot."

Oh, no! Stolen again? They gotta pay attention out there. We steal it from them; they steal it right back. Ai-yai-yai. The good news is that we're able to keep the ball down there. The bad news is we can't score.

Wait. . . . Are my eyes deceiving me, or did Wendy just pass the ball to Tara? That's what it looks like, unless I missed something.

"Nice pass, Wendy. We need more of that."

All right, Tara, let's do something good with the ball now. If Tara doesn't make a good play, I have a feeling Wendy won't be passing it to her anytime soon.

Great Steal

Uh-oh! Here comes a sea of red. How'd that happen? Guard the goal. Guard the goal! They're sweeping to the left. Come out to the top of the box. Guard the left side. Watch the angles. Who's dribbling? Number 12. Are you a shooter, number 12? Are you a passer? Who're you gonna pass it to? Watch for 22 behind her. Looks like 12 is setting 22 up. Anybody on the right? Nope. Here comes number 3, and 11 is close behind, too. They're all left. Guard the line. Cut off the angle. A pass off to the right. Who's that? Number 15? Where did *she* come from? Watch her feet. She's moving in fast. Watch her eyes. She's looking high. Now left. Gotta beat her to the spot. Stop the ball. Stop the ball. She shoots. High to the left. I knew it! Not in my house! Get it out to Tara and Wendy downfield.

We desperately need a goal. I don't even care if we win, as long as we can get a tie and stay in the hunt for the play-offs.

Finally! It looks like we got something going. Tara's got it wide open in the middle of the field.

"Go, Tara, go!"

Uh-oh. Here comes a red shirt from the other side. Man, she's moving fast.

"Tara, watch out!"

Too late! Tara's down in a pile of skinny legs. Is she all right? Play stops. Everybody takes a knee. She's up on her feet with the coach, but she's hobbling around. Not good. She's our best shooter.

Maybe she can just shake it off. Uh-oh, she fell again. Maybe not. Oh, jeez, Coach has to carry her off the field? What are we gonna do?

"Carly, you're in for Tara. Lindsey will finish the game at goalie."

Wait a second. . . . Did he just call my name? To replace our all-star Tara? He did say Carly, right? I point to my chest, and he points toward the field and screams, "Yeah, you, Carly. Get in there!"

Oh, man, the butterflies are dancing in my stomach big-time. Bummer I'm not guarding the goal, but I'm glad I'll get to touch the ball more; at least I hope so. Lindsey will be fine, but me . . . well, let's just say I haven't played anything but goalie for most of the season.

Here we go. Not much time left on the clock. Let's get something going. Tara was the striker, so I guess Wendy will be the striker now and I'll be the winger. Great. That means I have one job: get the ball to Wendy so she can shoot.

"Good steal, Megan. Look over here. To your left. Pass it off. I'm open."

Uh-oh, the ball is loose again. I chase it down and get to the middle of the field. Defenders are closing in on me. Where's Wendy? I kick a shot up ahead to her on her left side. Now *do* something with it, Wendy. That's it. That's it. Watch the double-team. Watch the double.

"Here comes help, Wendy. I'm here. I'm here. Behind you."

Oh, no, stolen again! Get downfield. Who's got the ball? Who's got the ball? Red number 9. One of their slower dribblers. Take it from her. Megan's playing her tight. I'll give her some help and we can double with a trap.

"Trap! Trap! Left side, Megan! That's it. Yeah!"

Our ball. Nice double-team from Megan. I got it. Get downfield.

Red shirts are coming. Can I get a pass to anybody in front of me? Wendy is way down near the goal. Too far. Too risky a pass. Maya is just up on my right. I forgot she was even playing. She usually just disappears into the background, but it looks like she's open, so she's getting it.

"Go, Maya, go! Get to the middle."

Maya's moving the ball nicely. The red shirts have been all over Wendy, leaving Maya open. Uh-oh. Here come a couple more red shirts. What is Maya doing? Is she blind? Stop looking at the ball, Maya, and look at your teammates!

"Maya, look up. Look ahead to Wendy. She's open."

Back to me? Wasn't expecting that, but neither was the other team. The goal is getting closer. Oh, man, I haven't shot in a while. Where's Wendy? She's got a cannon in her foot. Maybe she can get a better shot. I'll take a page out of the other team's playbook. Fake the shot and then pass it to Wendy. The goalie is cheating to the left. Wendy's coming on the right. Dribble . . . dribble. Not yet . . . not yet . . . not yet. NOW! Pass it to Wendy and . . .

"GOOOOOOAAAAAAAAAAAALLLLLLLLLLLLL!"

Tie game. Wow, I think everybody touched the ball that time. Cool!

"Alone we can do so little; together we can do so much."
—Helen Keller

CRACK-CRACK-CRUNCH

"COME ON,

Gillian, let's see that back handspring! You did it on the floor no problem. You did it on the low beam no problem. Now let's see it on the high beam!"

Four inches wide. Four feet high. Sixteen feet long. The balance beam. The sixteen feet long I have no problem with; it's the four-feet-high and four-inches-wide part that worries me. So far it's been easy because we've been doing stuff forward, but now we have to learn to go backward to move to the next level.

Every time I get up here, I have to calm myself down and relax. My heart starts racing and leaps up into my throat. My palms get sweaty. My head starts throbbing. My vision gets blurry when I look down. My calf muscles start twitching, and I get chicken skin everywhere. I try, but I never relax. I always feel like I'm gonna break a bone. Or two. Or ten.

"Come on, Gillian, let's go!"

Let's go. The two words Coach always uses to kick me into gear. The two words that mean it's time to say good-bye to another fear. I mean, that's all gymnastics is really about: fear. Fear of not doing something right. Fear of embarrassing yourself. Fear of breaking something.

My first-ever backflip years ago was kind of freaky, because my body had never done that before. Once my feet left the ground, though . . . oh, man . . . it was like my body just knew what to do. Before I knew it, I was on my feet, and Coach was clapping up a storm and shouting, "Yeah!"

Coach is clapping again now—not for what I just did, but to help me do what I need to do.

"Come on, Gillian. Practice is almost over. It would be so awesome if you could end it on a high note. I know you can do it."

I *can't* do this. I need more practice. Maybe I can do it tomorrow. Or next week. Who am I kidding? I'm just not ready. I say this to Coach, and he just looks me in the eye and says, "Yes, you are. Let's go!"

I was one of the first ones in the class ever to do a backflip because I didn't care if I fell. When you're five years old, you don't think about that stuff. But now . . . it's a different story. Our team has done lots of meets and competed in lots of events, so we've all seen some pretty crazy stuff. I've seen girls fall off the beam and twist their ankles, break their wrists, and land on their heads. The worst, though, was seeing this one girl fall off the beam and try to break her fall with her arm. Well, she did break her fall. And her arm, too. I remember it like it was

41

yesterday. Run-run-run; round-off; back fl— . . . *CRACK-CR-CRACK!* She started her flip, but her hands never touched the beam. Everything happened so fast, but when I heard that sound . . . that bone snapping—UGH . . . I told myself, *I'm never doing one of those up there.*

"All right, Gillian, the clock is ticking. If you're not gonna try it, let me give one of the other girls a chance."

I tell Coach I want to practice on the floor, so I hop off. Before I can move over to the larger mat, he tells me, "You're still going to try it today, though."

Maybe. Sabine's up on the beam now. She can do back hand-springs up there no problem. I wish I could do that. She's younger than most of the girls at this level, but she has no fear whatsoever. She just throws herself through the air no matter what she's doing. That's why she's moving up so fast. You should see her on the bars. When she gets spinning, it looks like she could launch herself into orbit at any minute. Coach usually has to have her slow down because she goes so fast. It took me a year to go from level five to six, and she's already gone from four to six in less time than me. But I'm not jealous at all. Hey, good for her. If you work hard, then you should move up. And, boy, does she work hard. It'd be real easy for a lot of us not to like her, but she's totally cool, because she's just this funny little ball of energy.

"How we doing over there, G? You're up next after Amelia," Coach says. He guides her through a back walkover, because she just started on her backward skills.

When it comes to certain events, we all have our favorite and least favorite. Amelia loves the floor but hates the bars. Sabine loves the beam but hates the floor. I'm the exact opposite.

It looks like Amelia is almost done, so I better get in another quick run to get ready. Run-run-run; round-off, aerial cartwheel; backflip, backflip, backflip. Stop. Whew, that was fun.

"Gillian, let's go!"

Yeah, G, let's go. I hop up onto the beam and do a quick run-through of everything I know going forward. Cartwheels, walkovers, jumps. Easy. No problem.

"All right, now let's see it backward," Coach says. He stands way off to the side, letting me know he isn't going to spot me. I stare down at the beam, and into my head pops a picture of bone poking out of flesh, while into my ears pops a loud *CRACK-CR-CRACK*.

What if I fall? I can't see where my feet are gonna land . . . so what if I fall off and break my arm? Or something else? Coach can't say it won't happen, because I've seen it happen.

"I can't do this, Coach. What if I fall?"

"So you fall. It won't be the first time you've ever fallen, and it won't be the end of the world. If you don't at least try, then nothing will happen. Is that what you want? You've been making great progress so far. Do you want to stop right here, or do you wanna move up?"

Of course I wanna move up. I need to move up. I can do all the skills in the other events, so I need to move up. I can't let this hold me back. Come on, G. If little Sabine can do it, what do *you* have to be afraid of?

"I don't understand, Gillian. You do back handsprings on the floor no problem. I mean, you're one of the best. If you can do it on the floor in a straight line, then you can do it on the beam. It's the same thing. Just pretend it's the floor."

Easy for you to say, Coach. That's not what I think about when I think about the beam. All I can think about is . . . that sound. There goes Sabine on the uneven bars, swinging away like she's launching herself into space again. The girl's fearless. Look at that smile on her face. It looks like she *wants* to launch herself into space. Come on, Gillian, if little Sabine can do it, there's no reason you can't.

All right, let's give it a shot. Close your eyes. Pretend like you're on the floor. Don't think about being on the beam. Don't worry about falling—

Oh, man! As soon as I say don't think about it, of course I think about it.

Try something new. I need to get that sound out of my head. Every time I look at the beam, it echoes through my eardrums.

I lift my eyes off the beam and let them wander around the gym. Everyone has stopped. Some of the girls are hanging out on the mat, cheering me on. The rest are hovering around the snack bar. The popcorn machine is popping a fresh batch, and Sabine is wedging herself up front for a fresh bag. The bags start filling, and soon Sabine and the other girls are on the mat, cheering me on between cracks and crunches of fresh popcorn.

"Come on, Gillian." *CRACK-CRACK-CRUNCH*. "Let's go!"

Coach tells the girls to keep the noise down, but I say, "No, Coach, let 'em crunch as loud as they want."

The louder the better. I'd much rather hear popcorn crunching than—

Come on, G. You can do this.

All right. Like Coach says, "LET'S GO!" Deep breaths. Arms up. Swing arms back. Arms behind head. Arch back. See the ceiling. Jump. Feet off the beam. Flip. Find the beam. See the beam. Hands on beam. Whip legs around. Keep feet straight. Whip feet over. Right foot, touch beam. Left foot, touch beam behind right foot. Stand. Arms up. Done. Smile.

Coach starts clapping, and the others join him.

"Great job, Gillian! I knew you could do it. How'd that feel?"

I hop off the beam and plunge my hand into Sabine's bag.

"Great! Now I'm hungry!"

**"Have fun, always set goals,
but never set limits."
—Shannon Miller**

A
MOUNTAIN
OF WOOD

"PAPER OR WOOD?"

Kyoshi asks me.

This is it. The last test before I get my brown belt. I've already earned the belt, but I want to break a board.

"Wood. I wanna punch wood."

"Are you sure you want to do a reverse punch, Candace? You might have a better chance with a side kick. Your legs are very powerful, you know," *Kyoshi* says.

"A punch. I wanna do a punch," I tell him, trying to catch my breath. Ever since I saw Nick try to punch through a board during his brown belt test, I've been waiting to try it during mine. He couldn't do it, but I probably can. I always beat him whenever we spar.

So far the test has been easy. I almost missed a few techniques when I had to count off all sixteen, but *Sensei* Jenkins asked if I was forgetting a strike, and of course I forgot the one I always forget: the ninja strike. I don't know why I forget it, because it's so easy to remember. Fold your arm so only your eyes show from behind your elbow, and then STRIKE and return to the first position.

My H-forms were pretty good. I hesitated a couple of times because I didn't want to mess up, but *Kyoshi* said to let the body do what it's been trained to do and not let the brain think too hard about it. Kind of like chewing your food. If you think too hard about it, it becomes hard to chew, but when you just do it, it's easy.

My kicks were nice and crisp, like *Kyoshi* taught me, but my legs are a little tired now from all those hops. Whenever I saw somebody else doing their test, I always thought that was the easy part, because you're just hopping over bodies lying on the floor. Hop. One body. Hop. Another body. All the way to the end of the *dojo*. Ten bodies total. Frontways down and back. Then sideways down and back. Yeah, it looks easy, but, man, is it tiring. I thought my leg muscles were gonna pop.

I had a feeling this would happen. That's why I wanna do a punch to break the board. I've been working on my arm strength with Dad. He's been doing push-ups with me so he can stay in shape. We're both up to fifty straight, although his fifty look a lot better than my fifty. He usually keeps going and has me try to keep up. I can't go as long as he can, but I'm getting there. Since we've been doing them together, I have noticed that I can punch a lot longer and my arms don't get tired as fast.

"OK, Candace, while *Sensei* Jenkins gets your board, you get to answer some questions from your fellow students. Ready?"

I nod to him and tug on my green belt. I'll be glad to get my brown one.

"Devin, do you have a question?"

"No, *Kyoshi*."

"Sebastian, do you have a question?"

"No, *Kyoshi*."

"Come on, class. I know you have questions. I know all of you have something swimming around in those young, sharp minds. You can ask her anything you want to. You know the drill," *Kyoshi* says, walking in front of everyone seated on the floor.

"Jessica. Do you have a question?"

"Yeah. I mean yes, *Kyoshi*. What's your favorite color?"

"Blue, because I love the ocean."

"Adrian, question?"

"What's your favorite animal?"

"Dolphins, because they're playful and smart like me."

"Miranda, question?"

"Why did you take karate in the first place?"

I've been doing this for so long now that I haven't thought about that in a while.

"Well, there was this girl about my age on the news a while back who got taken just a block from her house, and I didn't want that to happen to me. What else? Oh, yeah, and I like to kick stuff."

BREAK A BOARD

"Yeah, Candace, we know you love to kick stuff," *Sensei* Jenkins says with a smile. She has the board behind her back.

"One more. Nick, do you have a question for Candace?"

"How far do you wanna go in karate?"

That's easy.

"I want to keep going until I can beat *Kyoshi*."

Everybody laughs. I'm serious, though. I know *Kyoshi* has lots of notches on his black belt, and I want what he has plus one more.

"Very good, Candace. I look forward to that day as well, and I mean that. I have no doubt that there's lots of energy still untapped in that little body of yours," *Kyoshi* says, taking the board from *Sensei* Jenkins.

"Are you ready?" he asks, getting into position. *Kyoshi* and *Sensei* Jenkins kneel on either side of me with the board held between them.

This is it. Break a board with your fist.

"You can do this, Candace. Pick your spot. Punch through the board. Stay sharp. Stay focused."

Right. Stay sharp. Stay focused. Easy to say; hard to do. No matter how many times *Kyoshi* says it, my mind always disappears a little bit. But if my fist is gonna break this board, that's what I need to be: sharp and focused.

"Don't forget your 'kiyai' when you punch. I want to see you channel that power," *Sensei* Jenkins adds.

Right. Stay sharp. Stay focused. Pick your spot. Punch through the board. *"Kiyai"* to release my energy. A lot to remember.

WITH YOUR FIST

STAY
FOCUSED

"Come on, now. Measure it out so you can get good power. Take as long as you need. The board will be here waiting for you," *Kyoshi* says.

Stay sharp. Stay focused. Pick your spot. Punch through the board. Measure it out. Stand about here. No, no, no. Back up a little bit. Get closer. One step back. One step to the right. That's it. Good horse stance. Build a strong, sturdy base. Don't wobble. Exhale out. Inhale. Deep breath. Ready. Calm. Breathe with each heartbeat. Stay sharp. Stay focused.

"You can do it, Candace. Focus that energy," *Sensei* Jenkins shouts. The parents and my classmates start clapping to cheer me on.

Let's do it. Focus my energy. Start at the toes. Feel them tingle. Pull it from the toes to the legs. From the legs to the hips. From the hips to the torso. From the torso to the chest. From the chest to the shoulders, to the arms, to the elbows, to my right fist.

"KIYAI!"

All of my energy is released from my fist to the board.

OWWWWWW . . . that hurt! The board is still there between their hands. Did I even crack it?

"You OK?" *Kyoshi* asks me.

"Let me see your hand. Don't move." He touches my knuckles.

My fist is still trembling. It feels like somebody took a hammer to it. Everything sounds so fuzzy now.

"Everything's cool, Candace. Nothing's broken. You felt that, huh? That's a whole new kind of pain, isn't it?" *Kyoshi* says, his words cutting through the fuzz.

I just nod. The pain is pulsing from my fist to my toes and moving from my toes up to my eyeballs. Man . . . that HURT!

"That's OK, Candace. You did a great job. There is no shame in trying. I know you can do it. It takes time to break a board with a punch. Not many get it the first time around," *Kyoshi* says.

He pats me on the head, and my ears pick up my classmates and all the parents clapping for me. The fuzz starts to disappear, and the world stops wobbling. *Sensei* Jenkins gets my brown belt and hands it to *Kyoshi*. He holds it high for everyone to see.

"Congratulations, Candace, on achieving your brown belt. You worked hard for it, and you earned it. Before I present it to you, do you have any questions?"

"Just one. When do I get to try to break a board again?"

"In great attempts, it is glorious even to fail."
—Bruce Lee

MAKES ME
WANNA
HOLLA

"Ay, li'l man. Wanna run?"

Somebody talking to me?

"Ay, li'l dude. You hear me? I said you wanna play?"

The question bounces into my ears from the court just a few feet away. This baller decked out in baggy gear is bouncing a basketball with his right hand and clutching a water bottle in his left. I look around the court. The three-man game I was running is long over, and everybody else split. I stand alone on the court.

He shouts a little louder. "We need one."

And that one would be me. I tie up my laces, grab my ball, and head over.

Yeah, I'm in.

"All right. You wit' me."

Mr. Baggy Gear introduces himself as Mike but says to just call him Holla.

Holla? OK.

"So look here, kid. . . . It's me, you, Blue Shirt right here, my man in the green on the three-point line, and Syracuse Orange at the free throw line. Got that?"

I nod but notice that two of the players are wearing blue and standing not far from each other. Two of the other players are wearing green, one a Celtics T-shirt and one a Michigan State T-shirt with the sleeves cut off. So who's on my team again? I'll figure it out when we play. Syracuse Orange bricks two free throws and bounces right up to my face. His dark skin gets darker as he stands over me and eclipses the sun.

"Ay, yo, Holla, you sure you want this young cat on our squad?"

The words "young cat" might as well have been "little girl" when they were spat from his lips. He squeezes the ball between his long digits and laughs.

"He ain't no bigger than a flea."

Mike grabs the ball from him and heads toward half-court.

"Don't worry 'bout young dude, yo. We'll stick him on Pop and that'll even it out."

I glance over to see who Pop is. A pot-bellied white dude with a knee brace and goggles is on the receiving end of his pointer. You gotta be kidding. They think I can't even guard this dude? I might not be able to hang with most of these guys, but I could crack this cat in my sleep.

"I don't know, yo. Pop may be an old-timer, but at least he can shoot. Li'l dude'll be lucky to get a shot off. Especially if he tries coming my way," says Celtics Green, shadowing me now as well. My shaded eyes ignore him and focus on the rim in the background.

A couple of the other guys are starting to make noise, but Mike just starts dribbling the ball between his legs.

"Look, y'all wanna ball or not? We got nine; li'l man makes ten. Ain't nobody on the court but us, so unless somebody wanna sit and we run four-on-four, then li'l man is in. So let's go."

Let the torture begin. I just hope I can play with these guys. Most of them have like fifty pounds on me. Easy. I been playing as long as I can remember, and I've always done my thing with guys I played with, but they were always the same size as me. These guys . . . man . . . I feel like an ant in a forest.

"Holla, you wanna shoot for outs?"

"No doubt. Gimme the rock."

Mike, I mean Holla, stands at the top of the three-point line, bounces three times, and shoots the ball smoothly through the net.

Nice shot. I guess he can play.

"HOLLA! Our ball. You guys choose your basket," he says.

Celtics Green says they'll take the court we're at, so we walk over to the far court. Holla takes the ball at the top of the key and checks it. Everybody gets into position. Blue Shirt stands on Holla's right about five feet away. Michigan State parks under the basket on the right-hand side. Syracuse Orange stands under the basket on the left side. That leaves the left side near the top of the key for me. I drop down a little closer to the basket so that Holla can pass it to Blue Shirt standing next to him, but he calls me out.

"Li'l man. Come get it."

He tosses me the ball, and then somebody hits the fast-forward button. Pop rushes toward me on the left. Celtics rushes me on the right. A trap. Who's on my team? Who do I throw it to? Quick breaths. Gotta catch my breath. Arms dart in and out of my vision in a blur. And then: nothing. Celtics rips the ball right from my hands. Two of his teammates rush downcourt. One on the left. One on the right. He throws a baseball pass to the right side. Two quick bounces lead to an easy layup.

"One-zip," Celtics says, smiling in my face. "This is gonna be too easy," he adds.

I feel all eyes on me as I check the ball into Blue Shirt. Sneakers shuffle. Bodies bounce. I try to lob the ball to Michigan State, who's in the same position as last time. The lob isn't high enough for him, but it's low enough to steal. The other team's blue shirt grabs it in midair and flings it to Celtics, who races in for an easy jam.

"Two-zip," Celtics shouts for all to hear as he races back upcourt.

"Bounce pass, kid! Why you throwing me lobs?" Michigan State yells, motioning a bounce pass with authority.

I definitely can't play with these guys. They're way too big for me. They move too fast. I move too slow. I'm too small. . . .

Before I can even gather my thoughts, Pop has the ball and drains a long-distance three right in front of me. Three-zip.

That sparks a fire in Holla's eyes. The moment he gets the ball on the inbound, he pushes it up, stops at the free throw line, and splashes a picture-perfect J.

"HOLLA! Three-one."

Now I see why they call him Holla.

"Li'l man, come here," Holla hollers at me.

I hang my head and jog over.

"Let me ask you something, kid. What's the dealy, yo?"

What deal?

"You funny kid. 'What deal?' Listen, I was the first one here, and I saw you running things in that three-man on the other court before we started balling over here. I saw you breaking ankles and splashing J's. So I'm asking you now, what's the deal?"

Uhhh. I don't know.

"You don't know?" His eyes bounce between me and the court as he stands over my ear with his massive right arm slung over my shoulder.

"Look, kid. We needed one more to run a full. I had my choice of either you or Pop. I know you small and all, but I picked you up instead of Pop because I saw you doing your thing-thing before and figured you had some game. But the way you playing now tells me you ain't ready for this. When you get the ball, you look like a deer in the headlights, and the other guys can see that. I mean, I used to be small just like you, but I *knew* I could play. Couldn't nobody tell me nothin' when I stepped on the court. You feel me?"

DRIBBLE. DRIBBLE. LEFT.

DRIBBLE. DRIBBLE. RIGHT.

DO I HAVE GAME?

"Yo, you done with the powwow over there?" Celtics shouts from half-court.

He's really gettin' on my nerves. I never did like the Celtics.

"On the real, kid . . . *I* know you got some game in you. The question is . . . do *you*?"

Do I have game? Yeah, but . . .

We exchange baskets, and the score stands four-two. Their ball. I chase Pop around so many screens I'm starting to get dizzy, but I'm not gonna let him get an easy shot. If there's anything I hate, it's somebody dropping a J right in front of me. My hard work on D forces a turnover that earns us a quick basket.

"Four-three," Syracuse shouts. "Good hustle, li'l man. Now let's see some offense," he adds, flipping me the ball.

All right. Where is everybody?

Blue Shirt's jogging on the left. Dribble, dribble, left.

Michigan State's coming up quick on the right. Dribble, dribble, right.

There's no defense set up yet. Syracuse is trailing me on the left. Celtics is behind me on the right. Holla? Where's Holla?

A tall blur whizzes past me headed straight for the rim. The D is still behind me, so if Holla is thinking what I'm thinking . . .

Holla flashes his eyes at me when he gets past Blue Shirt and raises his eyebrows toward the rim. Yup, he's thinking what I'm thinking. Dribble, dribble, flip. Alley-oop!

Slam dunk. "HOLLA!"

"Four up, podna," Holla shouts after flushing my lob. Perfect.

"That's what I'm talking 'bout, li'l man!" Holla says, giving me a hard high five on the way upcourt.

"Yeah, boy," says Michigan State, gripping my head and giving it a quick push.

Do I have game?

That felt good. Focus. Defense. Gotta go to work on my D. Pop and his screens are driving me crazy. Pick and roll. Pop and Celtics. Blue Shirt didn't step up to Celtics. Switch. Me and Celtics. Uh-oh.

Breathe.

Exhale.

Inhale.

Relax.

"Well, well, well. I got the flea on me. I been waitin' for this. Look at you, li'l man. You scared. I can see it in your eyes," Celtics says, holding the ball near the ground in the triple-threat position, his right foot nearest to me.

Exhale. Inhale. Sneakers squeak past. Bodies blur around us. Time stops. I'm here. He's in front of me. Don't be scared. What's he gonna do? Haven't seen him use his left hand. He likes to go right. Don't let him. Stay in front of him.

"You ain't ready for this, son. I eat cats like you for breakfast, burp, and then do it again," he says, still holding the ball.

Blah, blah, blah. Ignore the words. Focus on the hips. My eyes aren't leaving his hips. My older brother always told me, it don't

Words to Live By

What motivates an athlete when the game is on the line and there is no energy left in the body? What motivates an athlete to remain calm under pressure when others are buckling under it? What motivates an athlete to step into the arena in the first place and believe he can hang with his competition? What motivates an athlete to constantly challenge herself when there is no competition but herself? What separates a great athlete from just a good one? Ultimately, the answer to all of the above is very simple—the mind. The body does what the mind says, and if the mind believes the body can do it, the body will respond in a positive way.

This was the inspiration behind the stories you've just read. As a lifelong athlete myself, I've learned that my greatest success comes when my mind and body are working together. When the going gets tough, my "inner coach" kicks in and tells me I can do it—and I do.

Throughout my life, the words of people I've admired have helped me overcome many obstacles and inspired me to achieve my own goals. Some of these words have motivated my mind to be strong and not give up, while others have opened me up to new ways of thinking and allowed me to grow as a person. There were also plenty that simply reminded me that, like everyone else, I'm human and not a machine, and it's OK to make mistakes.

In this book, I've created a collection of six short stories centered around some of my favorite quotes that I hope will inspire and motivate you. The stories cover four team sports and two individual sports, and each story focuses on a unique trait that allows the athlete to succeed.

Since different sports have different energy and rhythms, I photographed each in a unique way; the nostalgic feel of football is printed in sepia tone, while the kinetic energy of soccer is shot with bright colors. The direct simplicity of karate is shot in straightforward black and white, while basketball

is given a similar treatment, focusing more on shadows and silhouettes. Overall, I wanted each story to have its own energy and feel to reflect the essence of each sport and the athletes participating in each.

Many of the lessons that I've learned in life have come from sports, but it's been other parts of my life where I have applied those lessons. As a writer and photographer who works alone, I have to have the same discipline and focus as a martial artist trying to break a board. No one is going to do my work for me, so I have to make time to do it on my own. As an author who often works with others to complete a book, I have to have confidence in my team to make the book a success. As a performing poet, I have to have the same confidence as a basketball player competing against bigger, stronger, and faster opponents. And as an artist, I have to be able to take on new challenges without fear, just as a world-class gymnast would. Anything I do to make my mind stronger will make me stronger as a person, and these inspiring words out of the mouths of professional athletes, along with others I've read throughout the years, have helped me achieve the success that I have today.

As kids, we are focused on learning to play the game, taking years to become very skilled at one sport, let alone several. As we get older, we learn how to compete against others. There is that one moment, however, when we realize that sports aren't about how we fare against others but how we challenge ourselves each time we compete. Many great pro athletes were just as talented, and some less so, than their teammates at a young age, but, ultimately, what helped them become great was how they responded to failure, mistakes, and difficulty. Inspired by words from coaches, parents, and other athletes, their strong minds pulled them through.

I hope that you, athlete or otherwise, will take these words to heart and apply them to your life to help you achieve whatever dreams you have or goals you set for yourself.

For all those who have inspired me with words on and off the field

Copyright © 2008 by Charles R. Smith Jr.

First edition 2008

Library of Congress Cataloging-in-Publication Data is available.

Library of Congress Catalog Card Number 2007936030

ISBN 978-0-7636-1445-4

2 4 6 8 10 9 7 5 3 1

Printed in Singapore

This book was typeset in Berkeley.

Candlewick Press
2067 Massachusetts Avenue
Cambridge, Massachusetts 02140

visit us at www.candlewick.com